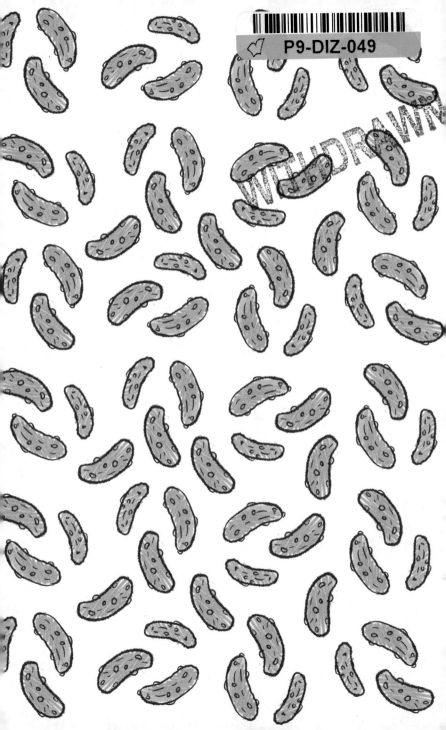

by Henry Winkler and Lin Oliver

HANK ZIPZER

the world's greatest underachiever

My Book of Pickles ...
Oops, I Mean Lists

by Henry Winkler and Lin Oliver

HANK ZIPZER

the world's greatest underachiever

My Book of Pickles . . . Oops, I Mean Lists

Grosset & Dunlap
An Imprint of Penguin Group (USA) LLC

GROSSET & DUNLAP
Published by the Penguin Group
Penguin Group (USA) LLC, 375 Hudson Street, New York, New York 10014, USA

USA | Canada | UK | Ireland | Australia | New Zealand | India | South Africa | China

penguin.com
A Penguin Random House Company

Cover and interior illustrations by Tim Heitz.

Published in 2014 by Grosset & Dunlap, a division of Penguin Young Readers Group,
345 Hudson Street, New York, New York 10014. GROSSET & DUNLAP
is a trademark of Penguin Group (USA) LLC. Printed in the USA.

Library of Congress Cataloging-in-Publication Data is available.

ISBN 978-0-448-48361-0   10 9 8 7 6 5 4 3 2 1

INTRODUCTION

Hi. It's me. Hank Zipzer. Maybe you've already met me. I'm in a whole bunch of funny books, you know. But in case we haven't already met, let me tell you about myself.

I'm not tall. In fact, I'm a little on the short side. But I make up for it in all kinds of other ways. Like I'm a good friend, especially to my best friends Frankie Townsend and Ashley Wong. And I'm pretty funny. Oh, I'm excellent at erasing, which is a very important skill because I can't spell anything right the first time. Okay, I can't spell anything right at all.

I go to school at PS 87 in New York, which is only one block away from my apartment building. My teacher is Ms. Adolf, who is the meanest teacher on the planet. That means Earth and every other planet, even ones they haven't discovered yet.

My mom runs a little restaurant called the Crunchy Pickle, where she is trying to bring luncheon meats into the twenty-first century. By that I mean, if you're ever there, don't order a sandwich. In fact, don't order anything. Just say hi and get a black-and-white cookie. (They're my favorite.)

My dad is a computer programmer and works at home. He likes that because he can go to work in his slippers. He has a lot of ideas about how well I should do in school.

Unfortunately, my brain has its own idea about how well I should do in school . . . which is not very. As a matter of fact, I have a learning challenge. That doesn't mean I can't learn, it just means I learn differently. I wish Ms. Adolf would understand that. The only thing she knows for sure is that school is no place to have fun. Ms. Adolf is allergic to laughter.

I have a younger sister named Emily who knows everything I don't know, and more. If she gets an A-minus, she cries. If I ever got an A-minus, I would celebrate until I was thirty-five years old. And then I would celebrate some more.

We have two official pets in the Zipzer apartment. We have a dog named Cheerio whose hobbies are chasing his tail and licking the bricks on the fireplace. As if you couldn't tell, Cheerio is an unusual dog. I'm pretty sure he has learning differences, too. Emily has an iguana named Katherine whose hobbies are hissing at me and stealing food off my plate. The one thing that Emily and Katherine have in common is that they both have scales—but don't tell Emily I said that. I also have a baby brother named Harry, but he's so little, I still put him in the "pet" category.

My life here in New York is pretty good. There are only two things that really bother me. One is that school is so hard. And the other is that Nick McKelty is always making fun of me. He's the bully in my class, and he never tells the truth about anything. He exaggerates whatever he says times one hundred. Frankie and Ashley and I call this the McKelty Factor.

I spend a lot of time being grounded for what my dad calls my irresponsible habits.

These include:

1. Losing my homework

2. Not doing my homework

3. Losing my jacket, socks, sweatshirt, gym shorts, and one sneaker

4. Forgetting my backpack at school

5. Leaving a half-eaten dill pickle in my backpack for two weeks. Okay, three weeks. I forgot it was there.

Oh, look at that! I made a list when I didn't even plan to. My brain does that without trying. I've been making lists since the second grade. In this book, I thought it would be fun to share some of my best lists with you. So get ready to read them and have fun. I even put in some blank pages at the end, so you can make your own. Try it. Your brain will thank you.

Here's a warning, though: Don't ever let Ms. Adolf get ahold of your lists. Oh, I know she's just a character in my books. But I'm telling you, it'd be just like her to jump off the page and show up in your room. If she does and asks about me, do me a favor and tell her I moved to Pluto. I'll return the favor some day.

So who's ready to have some fun and read my lists? You are? Good. What are you waiting for? Turn the page!

LISTS ABOUT ME

In this section, all the lists are about me. When you think about it, that makes sense—since the whole book is about me. By the time you finish reading these lists, I hope you'll want to be my friend.

Seven Reasons I Have to Make Lists in the First Place

1. When my brain is thinking, sometimes it gets all soft like mashed potatoes.

2. Making lists helps me remember things. Well, at least it helps me remember to make lists!

3. If I weren't making lists, I'd have no reason to use all my pencils.

4. I'd also have no reason to use my colored erasers.

5. Making lists gives me a chance to sit in my new desk chair, which spins around, and if you go fast enough, you can make yourself dizzy and then try to walk in a straight line across your rug.

6. When I sit at my desk and make a list, my parents think I'm correcting my math homework, which I couldn't even figure out in the first place.

7. Giraffes are my favorite animal. Oops . . . that belongs on a different list. See? That's why I have to make lists.

Me

This list was written by me, Hank Zipzer, when I was age seven and almost a half. I was supposed to be having quiet time at Jones Beach on Long Island, but I did this instead:

Ten Very Important Facts about Me

1. It's impossible for me to be quiet during quiet time. If I'm sitting, my leg bounces up and down. If I'm lying down, I keep flipping over.

2. My favorite meal for breakfast, lunch, and dinner is Cheerios with chocolate milk. I call them Choc-ios.

3. My hair sticks up in the morning when I wake up. I look like a porcupine.

4. I don't like to get sand in my bathing suit.

5. I don't know if the other word for sea is spelled *oshun* or *otion* or *oschun*. Anyway, it's big and blue and I don't know why.

6. I don't like to eat ice cream at the beach because the sun melts it faster than I can eat it and when it runs down my arm and I lick it, I get sand in my mouth.

7. I have twenty-four teeth and not one cavity.

8. I am better at watching sports than playing them, except swimming. I'm good at the backstroke.

9. I DEFINITELY do not like to get water up my nose.

10. My middle toe is the longest toe on my left foot, but I keep it mostly hidden in a sock.

This list was written on February 2 by me,
Hank Zipzer, while I was sitting in
Ms. Flowers's second-grade class:

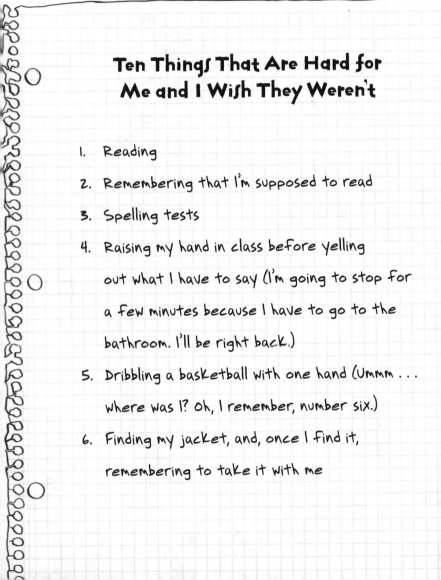

Ten Things That Are Hard for Me and I Wish They Weren't

1. Reading
2. Remembering that I'm supposed to read
3. Spelling tests
4. Raising my hand in class before yelling out what I have to say (I'm going to stop for a few minutes because I have to go to the bathroom. I'll be right back.)
5. Dribbling a basketball with one hand (Ummm . . . where was I? Oh, I remember, number six.)
6. Finding my jacket, and, once I find it, remembering to take it with me

7. Coloring inside the lines, or anywhere close to the lines

8. Adding and subtracting without using my fingers and toes

9. Keeping my notebook neat is easy. Knowing what to write in it is hard.

10. Getting my report card and trying to explain to my dad why nothing but "gets along well with others" is good

(Hooray! I finished! I'm going to high-five myself.)

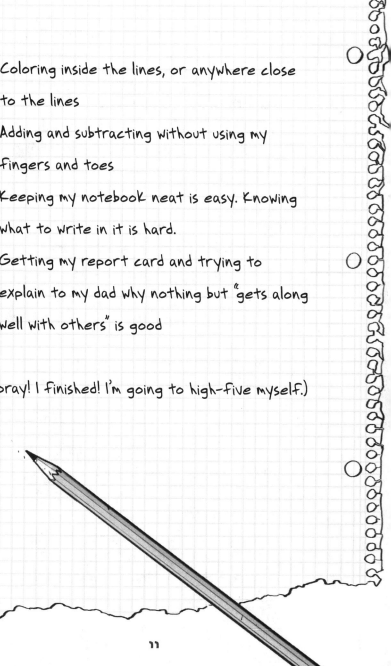

My dad always says how important it is for me to be a good athlete. When I failed at soccer and every other sport, the last thing I tried was Ping-Pong. I thought I was going to hate it, but I loved it! So here is Hank's tip for the day: You don't know if you're going to like something until you've tried it. This was the list I made before I tried Ping-Pong:

Ten Reasons I'm Going to Hate Playing Ping-Pong

1. I can't even see the ball as it whizzes by me.

2. I can hear it, but that's totally annoying—all that pinging and ponging gets on your nerves.

3. No one I know who is anyone I want to know ever even mentions Ping-Pong—except Papa Pete. But he talks about a lot of weird stuff, like whether green bell peppers taste the same as red bell peppers.

4. Every regular ball I know is made of rubber. I can't figure out what Ping-Pong balls are even made of—besides air.

5. Everybody in the Ping-Pong club was at least forty-eight, except for Sam, and he was five. I didn't see any other ten-year-olds there.

6. Everyone else I know plays dribbling sports. The only dribbling in Ping-Pong is the kind that comes from your mouth if you spill your 7UP.

7. You can't convince me that Ping-Pong is a real sport. I mean, when was the last time you saw an article about the World Series of Ping-Pong on the sports page?

8. My Uncle Gary likes to play Ping-Pong at the beach in his Speedos and orange rubber flip-flops. Enough said.

9. If Nick McKelty ever gets word that I'm a Ping-Pong player, he'll call me a pencil-neck, paddle-toting, weird-sport-playing geekoid. I'd rather not hear that for the rest of my life.

10. I don't think I really need to come up with a tenth reason, because I'm thinking one through nine are quite enough to make my point.

One Halloween, I went as a table in an Italian restaurant. Although I thought it was a great idea, I didn't plan it out very well. I couldn't even get through my front door. Nick McKelty made fun of me the entire day, and that made me really mad. Here are some other things I should have gone as, to get even with McKelty:

Nine Other Halloween Characters I Should Have Gone As

1. A nine-foot-tall emperor penguin that looks friendly but when it wraps its wings around Nick McKelty, it would squeeze him like the slimy fish that he is.

2. The ghoul from Zeon whose claws shoot out slime that would harden around McKelty and glue him to the playground, where the kindergartners would use him as a jungle gym.

3. A giant eyeball that squirts out eyeball gel, and when it lands on McKelty, removes every hair from his head. Everyone would call him Eyeball Head for the rest of his life. (Come to think of it, that name is probably too nice for him.)

4. A walking hand that is trained to pinch McKelty in the butt 24/7.
5. A crazed bowling ball that would follow McKelty around and knock him down every three and a half minutes. It would give new meaning to the word *strike*.
6. A zombie that lives in McKelty's closet and howls every time he opens it up. Wait a minute. The smell of McKelty's old gym socks would probably drive that zombie out of there and back to Zombieland forever.
7. Ms. Adolf in her all-gray outfit, who constantly gives McKelty a spelling test of really long words he's never heard of before, like *cornucopia* or *epiphany*.
8. I could keep going forever, so I'll stop now. (Okay, maybe just one more, because these feel so good I don't really want to stop.)
9. A human vacuum cleaner that would suck McKelty up and put him in a bag filled with carpet dust and iguana droppings. (Oh, Hank Zipzer, you are on fire! It's moments like these when I really love my brain.)

If no one else gives you a birthday party, I say do it yourself. Here are some of my basic rules for giving yourself a party:

Hank's Five Rules for Self-Party Giving

1. Only invite two-legged creatures with nostrils.

2. Eat your black-and-white birthday cookie first in case one of your guests decides that it's their favorite cookie, too.

3. Don't forget to give yourself a whoopee-cushion party favor, and be sure to put it under the big butt of any bully you meet. (I put mine under McKelty's.)

4. Make sure your balloon doesn't say "Get Well Soon" because all the grown-ups want to check and make sure you don't have a fever.

5. I was just starting to think up number five, but I got distracted by number two above. Once a black-and-white cookie is in your brain, it's not leaving until it gets in your mouth!

Ten Things That Are Better Than Having a Surprise Birthday Bowling Brunch

1. Nothing

I have actually spilled a root-beer float down my pants, and trust me—it's sticky and messy. I hope you never have to use this list, but just in case, here it is:

Five Ways to Get Out of a Bowling Alley without People Noticing You Have a Root-Beer Float Running Down Your Pants

1. Put your hands over your stomach, double over, pretend you're about to throw up, and run out.

2. Drop to the floor as if you're looking for a quarter that fell out of your pocket, and crawl to the front door.

3. Take your friends' drinks and pour them on you, too, and then tell everyone you're going to a costume party as a root-beer float.

4. Pull your shirt out of your pants, pull it down over your knees, and hop out of the room like a rabbit.

5. Bowl yourself out of there. Get a running start, dive belly-first onto the oil-slick lane, put your hands in front of you, and head for the tenpin. Exit on the other side of the pins. This is a little dangerous, so don't try it unless it's an extreme emergency—and then, don't forget to keep your hands stretched out in front of you.

pickles

are my favorite!

Most of the time, I'm not in favor of skiing on your butt. I think we'd all agree that skiing standing up gets you much more respect. Also, it's much easier on your butt. But once I was at the top of a steep, snowy mountain with no safe way to get down. The only possible way was to sit on my butt and ski. It looked very bad, but hey, I'm here talking to you and not at the top of some snowy mountain, so it worked.

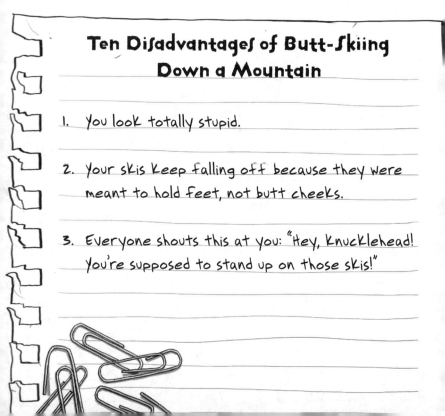

Ten Disadvantages of Butt-Skiing Down a Mountain

1. You look totally stupid.

2. Your skis keep falling off because they were meant to hold feet, not butt cheeks.

3. Everyone shouts this at you: "Hey, knucklehead! You're supposed to stand up on those skis!"

4. It's wet. No way can you keep your rear end dry when you're dragging it along in the snow.

5. You leave butt tracks, so even if people don't see you, they know you've been there. Enough said about that!

6. It takes a really long time. The human butt was definitely not built for speed.

7. The ski patrol stops you and asks if you're okay, and you have to pretend that butt-skiing is something you do every day.

8. Everyone snaps a picture of you and says, "I can't wait to post this on Instagram."

9. I wouldn't know this personally, but according to Emily, your butt starts to freeze up like a bag of frozen peas and becomes numb.

10. Did I mention that you look totally stupid? Yeah, well, that deserves to be said twice.

When I got the role of the King in our school play, *The King and I*, I was so excited I thought my head was going to explode. That was, until my pants fell down on the stage. I was so embarrassed I had to make a list of what could be worse:

Ten Terrible Things That Are Worse Than Having Your Pants Fall Down When You're in a School Play

1. My pants could totally fall down and just sit there around my ankles.

2. When they did, everyone would see that I have a rash on my inner thighs from the new laundry detergent my mom tried out.

3. I could start foaming at the mouth for no apparent reason.

4. The foam from my mouth could dribble down my shirt past the rash on my thighs, and land in a puddle on the floor.

5. I could slip on the saliva puddle on the floor and fall down, knocking myself unconscious in front of everyone.

6. While I was unconscious, my tongue could fall out of my mouth, showing everyone the mushy cream-cheese-and-jelly-on-toast breakfast that had molded itself, McKelty-style, into every little crevice on my otherwise pink tongue.

7. They could call the paramedics, who would come and refuse to give me mouth-to-mouth resuscitation when they saw the cream cheese and jelly on toast.

8. I would die right there in front of everyone in my class.

9. Which is what I wanted to do, anyway.

10. No, it couldn't have gotten any worse.

Seven Boring Things That Happen on a Typical Afternoon in the Zipzer Apartment (Okay, Very Boring, So You Might Want to Skip This List)

1. I come in from playing and hang up my jacket. I'm not going to tell you which closet because then you'd be so bored, you'd close this book and never pick it up again, which I don't want you to do because there are more funny lists coming . . .

2. My mom helps me work on a report about Why Tugboats Are Known as the Weight Lifters of the Sea. I won't tell you why they are, because . . . well . . . see number one above.

3. My dad watches *Jeopardy!* and gets in a bad mood because he missed the Double Jeopardy question where you had to name a small town at the base of the Matterhorn mountain in Switzerland. (In case you're wondering, the town is called Zermatt, a boring but true fact.)

4. Emily cleans Katherine's cage and insists on putting the dirty newspapers in my wastebasket instead of hers, which stinks up my room for a week.

5. We have garlic tofu burgers for dinner, which stinks up the kitchen for a week.

6. I go to bed hungry because I only pretended to eat the garlic tofu burgers.

7. I fall asleep and dream that Ms. Adolf has grown two more mouths and is yelling at me with all three of them. Eeeeeek! That's not boring, that's just plain creepy!

There are lots of people in my life who tell me things I don't want to hear, like "You're not trying hard enough," or "You're not responsible." Sometimes I daydream about things I'd really like to hear from people. Here are just a few:

Ten of the Greatest Sentences Someone Could Say to Me

1. Mr. Zipzer, your private roller coaster is ready for you now.

2. We're sorry to inform you that your sister, Emily, will have to repeat the fourth grade because she failed math, science, and language arts, and she really sucked at spelling.

3. Ms. Adolf will no longer be teaching at PS 87 due to her decision to ride a barrel over Niagara Falls.

4. The Mets baseball organization is happy to inform you that you have been drafted and will start at first base in the World Series.

5. Hi, Hank, it's Katie Sperling. Would you like to go to the movies Saturday afternoon . . . my treat?

6. I can't really focus on number six now because my head is still back with Katie Sperling, who is only the most beautiful girl in PS 87.

7. Okay, I'm better now.

8. Hi, Hank, it's Mom. I just bought a butt gadget, which we can attach to your baby brother, Harry, that will make his diapers smell like movie popcorn.

9. Your sister's iguana, Katherine, has just bought a plane ticket back to Brazil . . . one-way.

10. Hank, your mother and I are so proud of you.

Ten Secrets You Should Know about Me

1. Sorry, I can't tell you because they're all secrets.
2.
3.
4.
5.
6.
7.
8.
9.
10.

LISTS ABOUT MY FAMILY

Nothing the Zipzer family does is regular. Other families do normal things, like go to the zoo or drive to the beach or visit an aunt or an uncle in another state. But not us. When we take a road trip, we wind up in a van with nine Chinese acrobats. When we throw a birthday party, one of our guests is a hairy spider. When we have a new baby, we come very close to naming him Cutie Pie la Rue. It's just the way we are.

Here are some lists that will prove my point that the Zipzer family is just a touch crazoid:

Eight Words to Describe
My Family

1. I think we have to start with *weird*.

2. You might say, *fun-loving*, except for one of us isn't. Her name starts with an E, and the other letters are M-I-L-Y.

3. *Short*, and by that I mean, we don't play basketball.

4. *Book readers*—that would be three of us. *Learning challenged*—that would be one of us.

5. *Pickle lovers*—especially me and my grandpa, Papa Pete. We have been known to eat dill pickles until our lips pucker.

6. *Funny.* Even my dad, who can be a major grump, has a favorite joke. When I ask him, "How do you feel?" he says, "With my fingers."

7. *Warm.* I mean that in the hugging way, not in the "I need an extra blanket" way.

8. *People who see their glass as half-full rather than half-empty.* I just wish I didn't spill mine everywhere.

Ten Annoying Things About
My Sister, Emily

1. She tells me all the time that she's smarter than me.

2. She *is* smarter than me. What could be more annoying than that?

3. When she lost her first tooth, she left it in a glass of water on the bathroom sink to see if it would grow roots like a potato does. By the way, it didn't grow roots, but it sprouted hair that looked just like hers.

4. When she eats, she makes so much noise it sounds like there's a garbage truck in her mouth.

5. We always have to watch her shows on TV, which are usually about reptiles laying eggs in the sand.

6. Her pet iguana, Katherine, camped out in my bottom drawer and shed a ton of scales on my best Mets sweatshirt.

7. She spits a little when she says any word that starts with an S or a Z.

8. She always points out that my socks don't match—as if I care.

9. She also points out when my shoes don't match, which I actually do care about.

10. When we ride in the car, she breathes out my window. Why can't she breathe on her own side?

My sister, Emily, has a pair of lucky socks that have pink monkeys on them. Once, I wore them by accident and they brought me good luck in my baseball game. Even though they were lucky socks, I still didn't want to wear them out in public. I mean, would you?

Ten Reasons Why I Wouldn't Be Caught Dead in My Sister's Monkey Socks (Or Anyone Else's Monkey Socks, Either)

1. Monkeys should live in trees, not on your ankles.

2. Socks should be white, unless you're going to your cousin's wedding, and then your parents make you wear black ones.

3. I have never seen one player on the Mets wearing any member of the animal kingdom below his knees.

4. If Nick McKelty, the bully of our class, knew that I had even considered putting on red and pink monkey socks, he would say, "There's Monkey Boy," when he saw me every day for the rest of my life.

5. Number four is such a horrible thought; it counts for number five, too.

6. When Nick McKelty gets tired of calling me Monkey Boy, he'll switch to saying, "Gonna eat bananas and hang from the lights by your tail?"

7. Actually, hanging from the lights sounds like fun, because I could drop banana peels on McKelty's head. (I know this isn't really a reason, but it sure is fun to think about.)

8. Let me remind you, these were *pink* monkeys on *red* socks. Is that not reason enough?

**I skipped nine and ten because my brain stopped thinking of reasons after number eight. It does that. There's no arguing with my brain. When it's done, it's done.

Have you ever tried to get your parents out of town so they'd miss your parent-teacher conference? I did. I tried to get them to go to a rock concert in Philadelphia. My dad wasn't crazy about the idea, so I made this list to convince him to go:

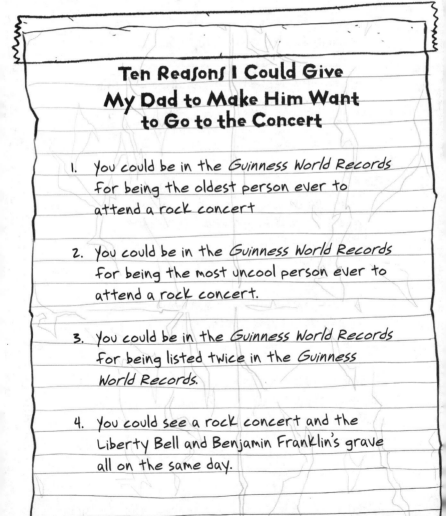

Ten Reasons I Could Give My Dad to Make Him Want to Go to the Concert

1. You could be in the *Guinness World Records* for being the oldest person ever to attend a rock concert

2. You could be in the *Guinness World Records* for being the most uncool person ever to attend a rock concert.

3. You could be in the *Guinness World Records* for being listed twice in the *Guinness World Records*.

4. You could see a rock concert and the Liberty Bell and Benjamin Franklin's grave all on the same day.

5. You could get a tattoo of a crossword puzzle on your upper arm muscle. (Oops, he doesn't have an upper arm muscle.)

6. You could get your mojo working. (I don't know if that counts, because I have no idea what a *mojo* is.)

7. You could bring back a whole bunch of souvenirs for Emily and me. That would make you feel so good—you always say it's better to give than to receive.

8. You could have a great time. Okay, it's not likely, but the point is, it *could* happen.

9. See below.

*** Sorry, all I could come up with were eight reasons. So get a pencil, go up to the top of this list, cross out the word *ten*, and write the word *eight*. Unless this is a library book. You never write in a library book. I made that mistake once and had to spend my next three weeks' allowance replacing the book.

Ten Things You Never, Ever Want to Hear Your Dad Say When He's Talking with Your Teacher (Or with Anyone Else, for That Matter)

1. I'm down with that.

2. You rock my world.

3. Want to see me break-dance?

4. Shake that thang.

5. Let's get funky.

6. Come on, come on, come on, babe.

7. Show me some love.

8. Who's your daddy?

9. Rock on, dudes!

10. I got my mojo working.

Memorize this list and make your dad take a solemn oath that he will never say these things in your presence or around anyone you know or anyone you may meet one day.

Ten Ways to Beg Your Dad to Say Yes When He Wants to Say No

1. Fall on the floor and pound the carpet, kicking and screaming. Whining is good, too.

2. When he says, "Stop that right away," stand up, apologize, and say you were just kidding.

3. Make sure you end every sentence with, "Pretty please with a cherry on top."

4. Tell him it will be your pleasure to polish every pair of shoes he owns or ever will own, even tennis shoes and flip-flops. And no, there is no tipping required.

5. Promise him this is the last thing you'll ever ask for except maybe a car when you're sixteen, and a new PlayStation on your birthday. Oh yeah, and the video games that go with it, but only four of them. Okay, five. But after that, nothing.

6. Swear to keep his mechanical pencils always filled with fresh lead. (WARNING: If your dad isn't a crossword-puzzle freak like mine, this one may not work so well.)

7. Try a compliment. Tell him that he's not going bald; he just looks really good in very short hair.

8. Trust me: Guilt works. Just mention that you know he loves your sister more than you, but it's okay, because you're fine with it. It only hurts a tiny little bit.

9. Don't try to scare him, but you might mention that if you don't get what you want, you may have to go lie down under your bed until you're forty-five.

10. Whimper like a puppy dog.

11. Go simple and just say please. **

**I can't believe that after all the time we've spent together, you're still surprised that there are eleven reasons on my list. It's me, Hank. You know I can't count!

The Seven Worst Places to Visit on a Road Trip

1. A factory where they use visitors to demonstrate how to use dentists' drills.

2. A tour of the trash dump where all the world's disposable diapers and used tissues go.

3. A visit to a school where opera singers learn to break glass while trying to hit their high notes. (I'd have to get earplugs for that.)

4. A factory where they make athlete's foot powder. (Oh wait, maybe that's a good thing because my feet are pretty sweaty.)

5. A guided tour through the publishing plant where they print my math textbook. (I'm getting a rash just thinking about it.)

6. A stop for an afternoon treat at an ice-cream store where the only flavor is fried ketchup.

7. A personal visit to the home of Ms. Adolf's twin sister. I don't know if she has one, but I can't even imagine it because the thought of two Ms. Adolfs will do damage to my brain.

8. Oh no, Ms. Adolf's evil twin is still in my brain. How do I get her out? What if she stays there the rest of my life? I've got to stop this list right now and go wash my brain out with soap. Hey, how do I get the soap up there? Maybe through my nose . . .

Five Places My Dad Actually Thinks Would Make a Cool Trip

1. A visit inside the world's largest mechanical pencil to see how it works. (Wow, that would be really dangerous. I mean, we could be rubbed out by the world's largest eraser.)

2. A field trip to visit the Dad's School of Boring Lectures about Why Homework Should Be Done Neatly and for At Least Twenty-Seven Hours a Day. (Holy macaroni, rash bumps are sprouting all over my upper arm just thinking about it.)

3. A spa just for dads where the only thing they do all day is fall asleep in a recliner in front of the television while scratching their butts and snoring. (Count me out on that one. All I have to do is put on my backpack, hike into the living room, and I'm on that trip.)

4. A crossword-puzzle convention where you do nothing but work on crossword puzzles and eat pretzels that are shaped like all twenty-six letters of the alphabet. (With my reading problems, I wouldn't be able to tell the difference between the B pretzels and the D pretzels because I get them so confused.)

5. A museum where they have a collection of ear hair from famous people, each in their own plastic bags.

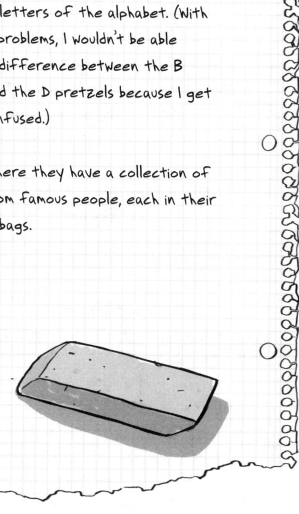

As I already mentioned, one of our Christmas vacation road trips ended up with us getting a ride from a troop of Chinese acrobats. We were in a big hurry to get home because my mom was in the hospital, about to have a baby.

Ten Useful Things You Need to Know When You're Stuffed in the Back of a Van Like a Sausage with Nine Chinese Acrobats

1. Really nothing, because the chances of you ever being stuffed in the back of a van with a human pyramid, two human coffee tables, and a human pretzel are slim to none. So, I've decided to blow off this list and substitute it with the ten things that flew into my imagination as we bumped along the snowy road . . . slowly.

2. The New List

3. If they built a bathroom in the back of this van, where would they put it? And boy, could I use it!

4. I wish I hadn't given those old Gummi Bears with the Life Saver frozen on them to Emily, because I would eat them right now.

5. I wish this were really a donut truck.

6. If it were, I'd get the classic glazed—or no, wait, maybe a jelly-filled one with chocolate sprinkles on top. No, wait, a lemon cream with powdered sugar.

7. I hope my mom is okay and that there wasn't a long line when she checked into the hospital. She hates lines, even two people long.

8. I hope there's a hot-chocolate machine on her floor, for her and for me.

9. I wonder if Emily's butt is still numb from the cold. Actually, I don't want to wonder that. *Thought, get out of my brain now.*

10. I wonder if babies have eyelashes when they're born.

11. Note to self: When I grow up, never wear a ski hat with red pom-poms. That is a big no-no.

12. These guys should go in the *Guinness World Records* for holding an uncomfortable position for the longest time ever. It's amazing that they did this for us.

13. Whoops. Did someone fart?

Ten Ways a New Baby Can Mess Up a Kid's Life

1. You're having a messy sandwich, you reach for a napkin, and you grab a used diaper instead.

2. I can't go on with this list. I'm still recovering from number one. (No pun intended.)

Before my baby brother was born, I wasn't sure how to take care of him. I came up with the idea of practicing on a baby pet. Here are some of the pets that wouldn't work too well as practice babies:

Seven Pets That Would Definitely Not Be Good Practice Babies (and Why)

1. An iguana (because I already have one of those in the house, and that is one more than any eleven-year-old guy should have to hang out with)
2. A goldfish (because I don't want to wear scuba gear and swim around the bottom of a fish tank all day)
3. A turtle (because it takes them an hour and a half to follow you into your room, and who has that kind of time?)
4. A hamster (because it pays no attention to you while it spends all its time running in circles around that stupid wheel)
5. A snake (because who wants to watch it digest a mouse for three days?)
6. A parrot (because if I want to hear a creature talk nonstop all day, I'll go into my sister's room)
7. A gerbil (because the fur on their face is not really something you want to kiss)

Finally, I settled on getting a pet tarantula. I named her Rosa and tried to see her as a practice baby brother. She didn't see it that way!

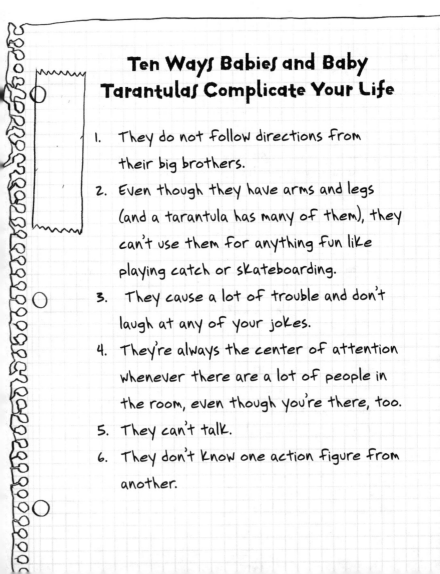

Ten Ways Babies and Baby Tarantulas Complicate Your Life

1. They do not follow directions from their big brothers.
2. Even though they have arms and legs (and a tarantula has many of them), they can't use them for anything fun like playing catch or skateboarding.
3. They cause a lot of trouble and don't laugh at any of your jokes.
4. They're always the center of attention whenever there are a lot of people in the room, even though you're there, too.
5. They can't talk.
6. They don't know one action figure from another.

7. They can't make a snack for you when you're watching TV and you don't want to get up in the middle of the best part.

8. They can't take a message when someone calls you on the phone and you're in the tub.

9. They can't change the radio station when the deejay is playing an annoying song.

10. So, I ask you, why have them around? Beats me.

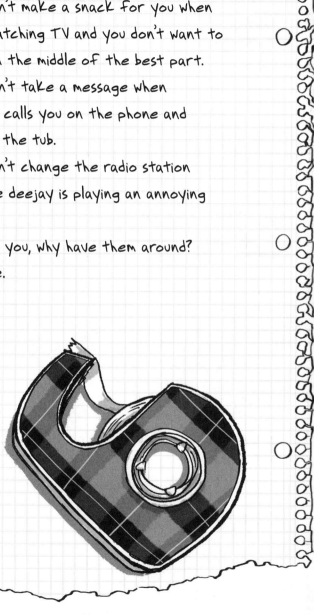

The Zipzer family spent a lot of time trying to come up with a name for our new baby. When you read this list, you won't believe your eyes. I told you my family was weird!

Ten Other Baby Names That Suck More Than Digman

1. Butt cheeks

2. Howie

3. King Mucus V

4. Madame Love Handles

5. Stinky

6. Rhino Haunch

7. Puddles

8. Cutie Pie la Rue

9. Hairball Le Pew

10. Farty Arty

LISTS ABOUT SCHOOL

To me, going to school is like climbing a mountain with no clothes on or riding a bicycle upside down or trying to look up a word in the dictionary. It's really, really hard. When my teacher is explaining a math problem, she might as well be speaking Russian or Greek. When we're practicing writing paragraphs, I spend more time erasing than writing. And don't even talk to me about science experiments. When I mixed two chemicals together in a beaker, it smelled like someone farted, and I had to spend the whole day trying to convince everyone it wasn't me.

What I am good at is lunch. I can eat a tuna-fish sandwich better than anyone in my class. I'm pretty talented in the potato-chip area too. I could improve in the cut vegetables part of lunch, although I love celery because of the crunch factor. Other crunchy foods that my ears enjoy are almonds, apples (red not green), Chinese fortune cookies, pretzels covered in chocolate, gingersnaps . . .

Oh, wait a minute. I'm supposed to be talking about school, not crunchy foods. Sorry about that. My brain and I apologize.

Five Good Parts of School

1. When the final bell rings and it's time to go home

2. Getting to see my friends

3. Hoping my picture goes up on the bulletin board as Student of the Week

4. Taco Thursdays in the cafeteria

5. Playing tetherball in the yard at recess

Five Bad Parts of School

1. When the morning bell rings and it's time to start class

2. Having to see Nick McKelty and all the food that's always stuck in his teeth

3. Knowing my picture will never be up on the bulletin board as Student of the Week

4. Fish-Stick Fridays in the cafeteria

5. Getting hit in the forehead with the tetherball at recess

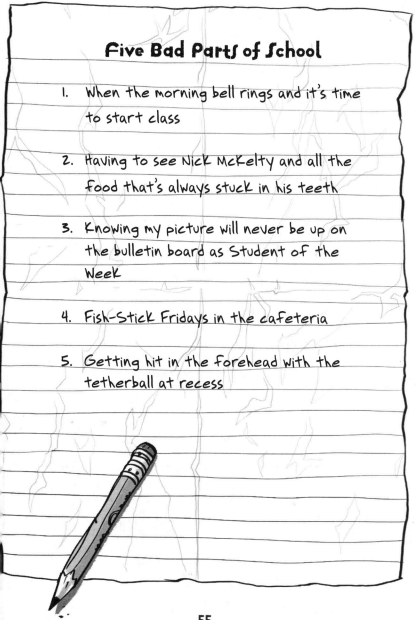

If I Were King of the World, Eight Changes I Would Make in School

1. Homework would be assigned only the eighth day of the week. (That's right—I do know there are seven days in the week!)

2. Cotton candy would be the mid-morning snack.

3. The teacher would read stories from nine o'clock to three o'clock.

4. Detention would be for teachers only.

5. They would show mutant-dinosaur movies during lunch.

6. Your pets could sit under your desk all day long.

7. You could wear your pajamas to school— except for the kind that have button-up flaps over the butt. Those are never okay.

8. Fill in your own here. I'm sure you've got a million changes you would make!

I made this list on the first day of school when Ms. Adolf gave us the assignment to write five paragraphs on what we did over the summer. Five paragraphs! I couldn't even finish the first sentence.

Ten Reasons Why Hank Zipzer Should Not Write a Five-Paragraph Essay on What I Did This Summer

1. Every pen I own runs out of ink.
2. My thoughts are controlled by alien beings that make me write in a strange language.
3. We couldn't go anywhere over the summer because my dog had a nervous breakdown.
4. I'm highly allergic to lined paper.
5. When I write, my fingers stick together.
6. If I sit too long, my butt falls asleep and snores, which keeps my sister awake.
7. Every time I write an essay, my dog Cheerio eats it for breakfast before I can get to school. So why try?
8. My computer keyboard is missing eleven letters—v, c, t, s, m, and all the vowels, including y and w.

The last two reasons were on the tip of my mind, but I just couldn't get them to the tip of my pencil.

So instead of writing an essay, I made my own Niagara Falls out of papier-mâché. I let my imagination go wild . . . on the project and on this list!

Ten Incredible Things That Will Happen After Everyone Sees My Niagara Falls Project

1. I won't just get an A on it, I'll get the highest A they've ever given in America.

2. Ms. Adolf will finally smile. (I wonder if her face will crack.)

3. They'll call an assembly for everyone in the school to see my project. Newspaper reporters will come. Television stations will bring their cameras.

4. I'll interview Frankie and Ashley on television. Maybe even Emily's little pal Robert. Hmmm . . . no, not Robert.

5. The mayor of Niagara Falls will come to shake my hand.

6. Principal Love will declare a school holiday in my honor.

7. I'll be called to the White House to show my project to the president.

8. The president will be so impressed, he'll pass a law that kids in the fourth grade no longer have to write essays.

9. Every fourth-grade student in the country will break their number-two pencils in half.

10. Just before they do, they will all write me letters to say thank you. I'll have to get a secretary just to answer my fan mail.

11. I will never have to clear the table again. Emily, on the other hand, will have to do it until she's fifty-six.

The Top Ten Things That Will Happen Because of My Bad Report Card (Except There's Only Seven Because That's All I Could Come Up With)

1. My parents won't be able to think of a punishment big enough for me. They'll have to hire an evil punishment expert like Darth Vader to think of one.

2. My sister and her iguana will laugh at me for months. And I won't be able to stop them.

3. I will have to repeat the fourth grade forever. Ms. Adolf and I will grow old together, and I'll turn all gray and rinkled like her.

4. My middle name will be changed from Daniel to Detention King.

6. The beautiful Kim Paulson will never let me walk to class with her again. I don't even want to walk with me—so why would she?

7. Here's the worst: Nick McKelty will tease me about being stupid, and he'll be right.

8. Did you notice that I skipped number five on the list?

9. And that I left off the w in *wrinkled*?

10. It's just more proof that I deserve those lousy grades I got.

My class was putting on a Multicultural Day
lunch and I decided to make enchiladas. But
first I had to make a list:

What to Buy at the Grocery Store to Make Enchiladas for Multicultural Day at School

1. Get all the things you need to make enchiladas.

2. I wish I knew what those were, but I don't have a clue!

3. Well, that's not totally true. I know it's not broccoli or octopus.

4. Octopus and cheese enchiladas. Barf-o-rama!

5. Help!

6. I'm stuck in this list and I can't get out!

7. How should I know what's in an enchilada? I'm just a kid!

8. Enchilada, schmintzalada! I'll figure it out later!

9. I know. You don't have to tell me. It's a stupid list. But hey, it was really funny at the time I wrote it. I guess you had to be there. And besides, I'm just a kid so I'm entitled to lose it once in a while.

We all know that you can't go on the school field trip without a signed permission slip, right? Then why did I forget mine under the Chinese vase at home? Because I'm Hank Zipzer, that's why.

Ten Creative Ways to Get the Permission Slip You Left Under the Chinese Vase at Home

1. I could go to the office, get a new permission slip, and sign my father's name on the parent signature line.

2. Then I could go to jail for the rest of my life for doing that. I think maybe I'll cancel number one.

3. I'll teleport myself right into my living room, get the permission slip, and beam myself back to my seat before anyone knows I was gone.

4. Before I do that, I'll have to invent the Time Travel Teleportation Body Mover Machine.

5. I'll pretend to have a horrible stomachache so the school will call an ambulance to take me to the hospital. I'll ask the driver to swing by my apartment so I can pick up the slip.

6. I could call Permission Slips R Us. Hey, maybe it exists. You never know.

7. I could pretend to be Mr. Sicilian, the other fourth-grade teacher, and walk right out the teachers' entrance. Oops, I'd have to grow a mustache first.

8. I'll learn to talk dog talk, call Cheerio, and ask him to bring the permission slip to school. *Hey, boy, arf-arf, bowwow, ruff-ruff.* Sounds right to me.

9. Hank, face it, you're not going. You're going to miss the best field trip of your entire childhood.

10. NO! I'm not giving up . . . not yet, anyway.

Once, in school, I was dying to see what grade Ms. Adolf had recorded for me in her roll book. I was so tempted to sneak a look, even though I knew it was wrong, that I had to make this list to keep me from doing it. (Oh, by the way, that plan didn't work!)

Ten Reasons I Shouldn't Look in Ms. Adolf's Roll Book

1. It's not mine.

2. I don't have her permission.

3. She's told us we can't.

4. No living fourth-grader has ever dared to look in there before.

5. I might see one of her cooties walking across the page.

6. The cootie could attack me and bite me, and I'd turn into a grumpy, gray-faced fourth-grade teacher with lint on my skirt.

7. What if Ms. Adolf set a finger trap in there that would snap onto my fingers and never come off?

8. I need all my fingers, in case one day I decide to play keyboards in a rock band.

9. Come on, Hank. Who are you kidding???? You know you're going to do it!

P.S. I know, I know. You don't have to remind me that there are only nine reasons on the list. I couldn't come up with the tenth. As soon as I do, I'll let you know. But don't hold your breath.

Ten Reasons Summer School Stinks More Than My Gym Socks

1. You can't dump summer school into a washing machine and make the stink go away.

2. Gym socks are soft and comfortable. Need I say more?

3. You can take a pair of socks off anytime you want. You have to sit in summer school from nine to three no matter what.

4. Socks come in all sizes. Summer school only comes in three sizes: tight, tighter, and cuts-off-the-blood-flow-to-your-brain.

5. Gym socks help me play. Summer school keeps me out of the game.

6. Gym socks absorb sweat. Summer school makes it collect between my toes. That's right—a lake between my toes.

7. Gym socks are perfect for playing toe basketball. But did you ever try to slam-dunk a classroom into your wastebasket?

8. There are many uses for gym socks—dusting your computer keyboard, shining your shoes, blowing your nose. I can't think of one good use for summer school.

9. You can use gym socks to make hand puppets to entertain small children. Summer school, on the other hand, would make them hide under the couch.

10. No matter how badly my gym socks stink, trust me—summer school stinks more.

We have this kindergarten friend named Mason. He's so adorable that we always want to pinch his cheeks. He hates that, so we made this list instead:

The Ten Cutest Things about Kindergartners
By Hank, Ashley, and Frankie

1. They have puffy cheeks.
2. They have the cutest little voices and the cutest little fingernails.
3. Every time you do a magic trick, they say, "Woweeeee."
4. Their sneakers are so small, they look like toys.
5. They like it when you help them.
6. They love sparkly things like rhinestones.
7. They say funny things like "buffalo" instead of "beautiful."
8. They're so light that when you pick them up, you feel strong.
9. They don't make fun of you if you can't read.
10. They look up to fourth-graders.

When I finished fourth grade, I was so happy . . . until I found out that I was going to have Ms. Adolf again for fifth grade. That would drive anyone to pick up a pencil and whip up a list.

Ten Things Any Normal Kid Would Say When He Finds Out He Has Ms. Adolf the Second Year in a Row

1. I'm dead.
2. I'm dead meat.
3. I'm dead rat meat.
4. I'm double-dead rat meat.
5. I'm double-dead rat meat with only one claw.
6. Wait a minute. Let me rub my eyes and check again, because maybe what I'm seeing isn't real.
7. Nope, it's her. Ms. Adolf in the flesh.
8. You can handle this, Hank. It's only a year.
9. That's 365 days.
10. Let me get out my calculator. That is 8,760 hours, 525,600 minutes, and 31,536,000 seconds.
11. I'm going to spend the next 31 million seconds with Ms. Adolf.
12. Oh, yeah. I'm rat meat times 31 million.
13. Stick a fork in me. I'm done.**

**I know, I know. This is more than ten things. But give me a break, will you? If you just found out that you had Ms. Adolf again, you wouldn't be able to count, either.

What Happens to People Who Don't Complete the Fifth Grade

1. You get to ignore the alarm clock and sleep as late as you want. How great is that!

2. You get to lie on the couch and watch TV all day. Wow, that sounds wonderful.

3. You get to eat pizza for breakfast, lunch, and dinner. Wow, why didn't I think of that before?

4. You get to play video games until your thumbs fall off. Who needs thumbs, anyway . . . you wouldn't have to hold a pencil anymore.

5. You get to see your friends whenever you want and watch movies on the computer. Yeah, that's the life.

6. Wait a minute. What am I thinking? If I slept late every day, I'd miss the morning. And I really like the morning, especially the smell of cooking waffles coming out of everyone's windows.

7. And about that all-day TV watching . . . come to think of it, it's mostly soap operas that are on, and everybody's yelling at one another . . . and if they're not yelling, they're kissing. Ick.

8. Pizza for breakfast, lunch, and dinner? Hey, I love pizza, but the thought of eating it three times a day every day is making me burp, and I haven't even had one piece yet.

9. And playing video games really gets boring after a while. And I don't want my thumbs to fall off. I like my thumbs. They really come in handy when you're giving a thumbs-up sign.

10. And about hanging out with your friends all day . . . well, that's not going to happen . . . they'd all be in school. That's where I should be!!!!!!!!!!!!!!!!

Picture this: my soccer coach asks the whole team to "take a knee" and "listen up" as he gives us his big speech about team spirit. I look like I'm listening, but here's what's really going on in my mind:

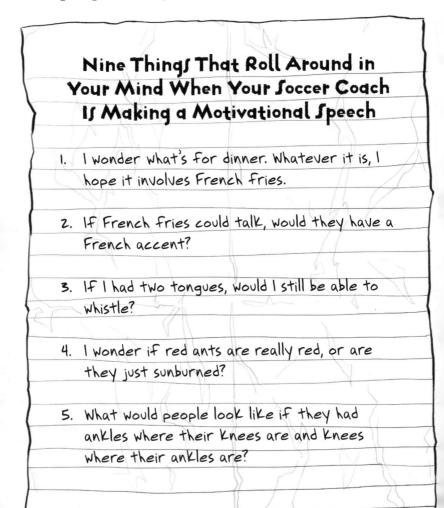

Nine Things That Roll Around in Your Mind When Your Soccer Coach Is Making a Motivational Speech

1. I wonder what's for dinner. Whatever it is, I hope it involves French fries.

2. If French fries could talk, would they have a French accent?

3. If I had two tongues, would I still be able to whistle?

4. I wonder if red ants are really red, or are they just sunburned?

5. What would people look like if they had ankles where their knees are and knees where their ankles are?

6. What's the point of hair growing in your nose? Is it supposed to keep the inside of your nose warm?

7. Will they ever change the name of New York City to old York City? I mean, it's really not so new anymore.

8. If pickles were blue, would I still like to eat them?

9. What if balls were square? Would they still—

"Zipzer, did you hear anything I said?"

"Oh yes, Coach Gilroy. Every word. And it is so interesting."

73

Ten Things That Would Be as Difficult as Me Getting a B-Plus on a Math Test

1. I could hold a rope between my teeth and pull the family minivan with the whole family in it (including Cheerio) all the way out to Aunt Maxine's on Long Island while singing "Yankee Doodle."

2. I could hop across the Manhattan Bridge upside down while standing on one hand, right into my favorite Chinese dumpling restaurant, and eat two dozen pork dumplings with my toes.

3. I could use a diving board to spring into outer space, where I would land on Mars and send back photographs of me doing the cha-cha with a bunch of Martian girls.

4. I could root for the Yankees to beat the Mets in the World Series.

5. (Nope, I could never do that. That's just not possible. Not ever.)

6. I could keep my sock drawer neat and organized.

7. (Nope, that's not possible, either.)
8. Okay, I could live in an igloo in the North Pole for a whole winter, eating whale blubber sandwiches on Wonder bread, wearing only a bathing suit.
9. Actually, that sounds more doable than getting a B-plus on my math test.
10. I can't go on with this list—not because I'm out of ideas, but because my father is yelling through the door that Heather Payne called to say we're meeting tomorrow morning before school so she can help me go over . . . yes . . . long division homework. Oh, Heather, will you ever get a life? Or more important, will you ever let me get one?

One day, Ms. Adolf missed school, which is something she never does. They told us she had thrown her back out—whatever that means—while participating in her favorite hobby. Ms. Adolf has a hobby? My brain went nuts trying to figure out what it was.

Eight Ways Ms. Adolf Could Have Thrown Her Back Out While Participating in Her Favorite Hobby

1. Maybe she was a contestant in the Strongest Woman in the World competition and was towing a jumbo jet down the runway by a rope tied around only her left ankle.

2. Maybe while scuba diving she was attacked by a giant squid that mistook her for a spiny crab (which, by the way, she is).

3. Maybe once the squid realized that she wasn't a spiny crab, he used three of his eight arms as a slingshot to fling her back to shore, where she landed on her back. Ouch.

4. Maybe she was bowling, and her fingers got

stuck in the ball, and she threw herself down the lane. (If you knock all the pins down with your body and not the ball, I wonder if that's still considered a strike?)

5. Maybe she's a rodeo rider and a bucking bronco bucked her off so hard that she went into orbit and landed on her back in New Jersey.

6. Maybe she was in a spelling bee and got so upset when she misspelled *receive* (like I always do) that she fainted and fell off the stage and landed on the world's biggest dictionary.

7. Maybe she was writing a Big Fat Red D on my last math test with such force that her whole back went into a spasm and all of a sudden half of her was facing frontward and the other half was facing backward.

8. Maybe she has a secret life as a ballroom dancer and was injured while doing a wild rumba turn with her handsome partner from Argentina. No, what are you thinking, Hank? That's way too cool a thing for Ms. Adolf to ever do.

Hank Zipzer's Nine Tips for Getting Your Homework Done Really, Really Fast

1. If it's math homework, skip the odd problems and only do the even ones. Tell your teacher that you're allergic to odd problems and when you do them your scalp itches like crazy.

2. If they're short-answer questions, take the directions seriously and give short answers.

3. If they're multiple-choice questions, don't stress yourself out worrying about which answer is right. Take your best shot and move on.

4. If you have to write a paragraph, remember that there's no law that says it has to make sense.

5. If you have to write an essay, well, sorry, but there's no quick way around that. Once, I told Ms. Adolf that I couldn't write the essay because I had so many ideas for it, I couldn't decide which one to write. (She didn't buy it, but hey, that doesn't mean it won't work for you.)

6. See number nine.

7. See number nine.

8. See number nine.

9. There's nothing wrong with skipping a few questions. See numbers six through eight as examples.

Ten Things You Can Do in a Motel Room When You're on Vacation Instead of Doing Your Homework

1. Lie on the bed and look up at the ceiling.
2. Flip over onto your stomach and bury your face in the pillow.
3. Lie on your right side and look out the window into the parking lot.
4. Lie on your left side and look at the wall with the painting of a sunflower on it.
5. Flip onto your back and check out the smoke alarm on the ceiling.
6. Flip onto your stomach and make snorting sounds into the pillow.
7. Lie on your right side and reach for the TV remote control on the nightstand next to your bed.
8. Flip onto your left side and click on the remote control.
9. Watch the TV screen light up with a whole menu of shows to watch.
10. Think about whether to do your homework packet or watch TV. (Is there really any question about this? Watch TV, of course!)

FRIENDS AND CLASSMATES

I am so lucky to have such good friends. Frankie Townsend has been my best friend since before preschool, when we were just a couple of babies who drooled all the way down to our belly buttons. Ashley Wong is our other best friend. She's a girl friend, but before you get all boy-girly about it, let me just emphasize that she's a *girl* who is also a *friend*. The thing I love best about both Frankie and Ashley is that they don't judge me, even though school is so hard for me.

Frankie and Ashley and I get along with almost everyone in our class at PS 87. Sure,

Luke Whitman is a major nose picker, and Katie Sperling gets a little too giggly sometimes. And Heather Payne, who is the smartest girl in the class, never lets you forget it. But we like everyone—everyone but one guy whose name happens to be Nick "the Tick" McKelty. He's a total bully who never stops bragging and picking on people, especially me. If you ever meet him, you'll recognize him right away because he usually has my school-lunch dessert stuck between his two front teeth.

Here are a few lists about my friends at school. I hope these lists are as much fun as my friends are:

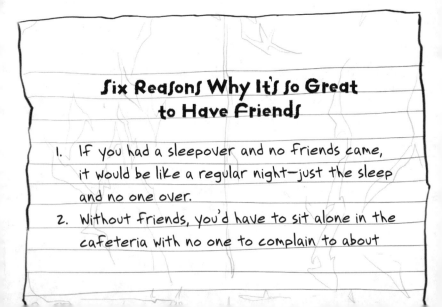

Six Reasons Why It's So Great to Have Friends

1. If you had a sleepover and no friends came, it would be like a regular night—just the sleep and no one over.

2. Without friends, you'd have to sit alone in the cafeteria with no one to complain to about

how stinky the fish sticks are.

3. If you had no friends, when the phone rings, you'd know for sure it wasn't for you.

4. If you were watching a scary movie, like *The Mutant Moth of Toledo*, you'd have no one to scream with. (Or throw popcorn at.)

5. If you had no friends, when you call a meeting in your secret clubhouse, only you would show up.

6. When you're having a down day, nothing feels better than being with your good friends. (I didn't mean that to sound all mushy, but it's true. Sometimes you've got to go with the mush.)

my best friends

The Four Best Things I Like about My Best Friend, Frankie

1. He's a great magician, and once, when Emily was being totally annoying, he tried really hard to make her disappear.

2. He makes the best ham-and-pickle-on-graham-crackers sandwiches. When I try to make them, they just crumble and turn into graham-cracker mush.

3. When I tell a joke, Frankie laughs so hard that he gets the hiccups . . . and doesn't care.

4. No matter what kind of trouble I get into, I can always count on him to help me out of it.

The Four Best Things I Like about My Other Best Friend, Ashley

1. She puts rhinestones on anything and everything. If you turn your back on her for one minute, you're going to have pink rhinestones on your gym socks.
2. Her grandmother makes the crunchiest wontons for after-school snacks, and Ashley always saves us some.
3. She's always got ideas for us to make money. Once, she found a quarter in a puddle on Seventy-Eighth Street. Too bad she also found a soggy French fry in the same puddle.
4. No matter what kind of trouble I get into, I can always count on her to help me out of it.

Eight Things That Are Hard for Me and Easy for Frankie

1. Spelling, especially hard words like what you call the person who lives next door to you. You know, your next-door nay-bor or is it neibor or neyber? I don't know, so don't ask me. (Frankie is a dictionary with a mouth.)

2. Remembering words to songs. (Frankie is a human karaoke machine.)

3. Learning how to play an instrument—except for the tambourine, and who wants to play that? (Frankie plays the sax and knows over ten songs by heart.)

4. Finding my backpack. (Frankie's backpack is where it belongs, on his back.)

5. Remembering phone numbers. (Frankie not only remembers phone numbers, he remembers area codes, too.)

6. Reading a map. (Frankie is a human compass.)

7. Writing a letter. (Frankie is the King of Thank-You Notes.)

8. Reading the program guide on the television screen. I am a total flop at that.

Nick McKelty is the King of Doing Mean Things. Here are just a few of the things he's done to me that I consider to be "truly rotten":

Eight Truly Rotten Things McKelty Did, Even Though There Were Way More

1. He sneezed a big wet sneeze into a Kleenex and then stuffed the tissue into my jeans pocket so I'd have to touch it. No kidding. He really did that.

2. He kept trying to trip me coming down the stairs, but his feet are so huge and he's so klutzy, he tripped himself instead.

3. He had his girlfriend, Joelle Atkins, call me on her cell phone, disguise her voice as Katie Sperling, and ask me to the movies. I didn't fall for it, since Joelle sounds like Barney the Purple Dinosaur, and the one time I spoke to Katie Sperling on the phone in the second grade, she sounded like a movie star.

4. He told me Heather Payne had poison oak between her fingers, and if I danced with her, I'd get it and then it would spread all over my body and even behind my eyelids.

5. He tried to switch my milk carton at lunch with one that he had kept in his desk for several days, so I'd drink the sour milk and get a horrible stomachache. Luckily, my nose sniffed out the problem before the carton reached my mouth.

6. He locked me out of the multipurpose room before play rehearsals. It's a good thing the director of the play saw my head bouncing around in the glass pane of the door as I frantically jumped up and down to see in. Fortunately, I was wearing my basketball shoes, which make me jump higher.

7. He wrote a letter to the director of the play as if he were me, resigning from the play for "personal reasons." He's so stupid, though—he signed his own name.

8. He tried to convince Frankie and Ashley to talk me into resigning from the play because he said the King of Siam should be played only by someone who is truly Siamese, and although he wasn't actually Siamese, he once petted a Siamese cat and didn't get an allergy attack, so he must be one-sixteenth Siamese.

My sister's best friend is this little worm of a guy named Robert. Robert wears a tissue box around his neck and knows too many facts, like that there's enough iron in the human body to make one nail. Once, when we were going to a birthday party at my Aunt Maxine and Uncle Gary's house at the beach, Robert wanted to come. We didn't want him to, so we made this list of excuses:

Ten Excuses We Could Give Robert for Why He Can't Come on the Trip

1. It's very windy at the beach. Robert could get picked up by the wind and blown out to sea. Okay, it doesn't happen often, but it could.

2. A flock of seagulls could mistake Robert for a large rodent and swoop down and carry him off to their nest. Okay, it doesn't happen often, but it happens.

3. Robert is a walking, talking encyclopedia of facts. My Aunt Maxine gets a rash if she hears too many facts.

4. My Uncle Gary gets a rash if my Aunt Maxine gets a rash.
5. There is only a limited amount of oxygen in the car and let's face it, Robert just sucks in too much of it.
6. Robert is so skinny he could slip through a crack in the seat, and we could lose him and never know it.
7. Robert has such bad allergies that the beach air would make his nose run so much there aren't enough Kleenex in all of Long Island to handle the slime.
8. I hear they are having an ice-cream birthday cake and Robert himself has told me many times (way too many times) that ice cream gives him mucus buildup.
9. He'd have to sit next to my weird younger sister, Emily, in the backseat of the minivan and—

Wait a minute. Hank Zipzer, look what you just came up with. Robert would have to sit next to my sister, Emily, in the car! THAT MEANS I WOULDN'T HAVE TO SIT NEXT TO HER!!

Robert, my man. Good news! You're invited to a birthday party!

I am always mad at Nick McKelty, but trust me, he deserves it. I spend a lot of time thinking up ways to get even with him for teasing me. You might say it's one of my hobbies. I made this list during a school field trip on an old sailing ship:

Ten Ways I'm Going to Get Even with That Rotten, Lousy Punk, Nick McKelty

1. I'm going to find all the creepy-crawly bugs that live on this boat and hide them in McKelty's dinner.

2. After he eats the bugs, I'll tell old Nick that the creepy-crawlies are probably having a great time feasting on his liver.

3. I'll hide Nicky Boy's belt and then get him to do a sailor's jig in front of both classes. His pants will fall down, and everybody will see his G.I. Joe underpants.

4. He'll be so embarrassed, he'll throw himself overboard.

5. I'll find a sea cucumber on the bottom of the river, which I happen to know are slimy and ooze purple ink. I'll replace his pillow with the sea

cucumber, and when he puts his big fat head down on Mr. Cuke, it will pee purple stuff up his nose.

6. No, I can't do that to a sea cucumber.

7. Maybe I'll just have to tell Katie Sperling that Nick rubs diaper-rash cream on his chapped kneecaps.

8. I'll tell the captain that the rash on his knees is scurvy and very contagious, so they'll have to lock him up in the ship's jail and throw away the key.

9. When he's asleep, I'll squirt whipped cream in his hand and then tickle his nose with a feather so when he scratches, he smears whipped cream all over his big, ugly face.

10. I'll put his hands in warm water while he's sleeping so he pees up a storm in his sleeping bag.

11. Numbers one through ten are all so good, I could never choose just one. I think I'll have to do them all.

12. I know this is more than ten, but I'm so mad I can't stop myself.

Ten Insults I'd Like to Say to
Nick McKelty When I See Him in the Hall

1.   Why don't you make like a tree and leave?

2.   What are you doing here? Did someone leave your cage open?

3.   I'd like to invite you someplace special. It's called outside.

4.   I hate to see you go, but I'd love to watch you leave.

5.   I thought they only allowed humans in here.

6.   Why don't you go to the library and brush up on your ignorance?

7.   Before I saw you, I was hungry. Now I'm fed up.

8.   I'm very busy now. Can I ignore you some other time?

9.   I'd like to help you out. Which way did you come in?

10. King Kong's calling you. He wants his face back.

* Feel free to vote and select what you would say to Nick if you were me.

You're not going to believe this, but Nick McKelty has the coolest cousin. Her name is Zoe, and let's just say she understands me.

Nine Ways Zoe McKelty Is Not Like Her Creepy Cousin Nick

1. She does not have brown cookie crumbs stuffed between her two front teeth and crusted around the corners of her mouth.

2. She does not call me Zipperbutt, Zipperhead, or Zipper Doofus.

3. She does not go around saying that her father is best friends with everyone from the queen of England to every guy in the Baseball Hall of Fame—even the dead guys.

4. She does not have a thick neck the size of one of those five-thousand-year-old redwood trees.

5. Her breath does not smell like burning rubber.

6. She does not lie about how she is the best at everything, including things she has never even done like pole-vaulting, bungee jumping, and camel racing.

7. When she laughs, she does not sound like a woodpecker with a stomachache.

8. Oh, yeah, and the main way she's not like Nick McKelty is this: She likes me.

9. There, I said it. She likes me!

On our sailing-ship field trip, I met a guy named Collin Rich. He seemed perfect in every way, and boy did I feel like a lowly worm next to him. But then I got to know him, and here's what I learned:

Ten Things You Wouldn't Know about Collin Just From Looking at Him

1. He bites his nails, too.

2. He pulls cards from the middle of the Chance pile in Monopoly.

3. He likes the Yankees better than the Mets. That made Frankie happy.

4. At night, he wears headgear the size of a flying saucer. That's how he gets those perfectly straight teeth.

5. His favorite fruit is prunes.

6. He only knows three knock-knock jokes, and two of them aren't funny.

7. He is scared of scary movies.

8. He is also afraid of iguanas.

9. He can't make himself burp unless he's had a Coke first.

10. He is one lousy bowler.

I showed this list to Papa Pete. He says it proves one thing: Nobody's perfect, even the perfect people.

Frankie, Ashley, and I built a haunted house for Halloween. It was so scary we even scared ourselves!

The Ten Coolest Things We Put in Our Halloween Haunted House

1. We hung the black light on the skeleton's ribs, so the entire bony dude glowed a creepy whitish-purplish color.

2. We tied all the rubber spiders onto Ashley's dad's fishing pole and hung it in the corner, so when people walked by, we could drop the spiders into their hair. That would make the hair on their necks stand at attention.

3. We recorded Frankie's scary howl into a tape recorder. Then we slowed the tape recorder down so when we played it back, the howls turned into spine-chilling shrieks.

4. We peeled grapes so they were the perfect texture for eyeballs and put them in a bowl of slimy egg whites, as if the eyeballs had just spewed their gooey insides into the bowl.

5. We made a human brain by boiling spaghetti noodles until they were mushy and mixing them with Marshmallow Fluff so the brain would stick to kids' fingers when they touched it. Nobody wants to walk around with gray matter stuck to their fingers.

6. We lined my old Mets hat with Saran Wrap and put the brain mixture in it. When kids stuck their hands in that hat, they would think someone took their hat off and their brain came with it. (I'm even grossing myself out now.)

7. We made a ghost out of Emily's bedsheet, and then we put a fan under it, so it would billow out and look like it was about to take off and fly around the room.

8. We went through three large economy-size bottles of ketchup, covering most anything you can think of with fake ketchup blood—including a roasting fork, gauze bandages, and an old undershirt of my dad's.

9. We saved the last bottle of ketchup to add a bloody spot to the ghost's chest area, where its heart would have been.

10. The last thing we made was too gross to even tell you about. Okay, I'll give you a clue. It involved real spiderwebs, human saliva, mayonnaise, and dust balls from under the couch. I told you it was gross.

LISTS ABOUT PETS

Our dog, Cheerio, is the greatest pet you could ever have. He's a dachshund, sometimes called a wiener dog, because he's long and low like a beige hot dog. He loves to spin in circles to chase his tail, which makes him look round like a Cheerio. There's nothing I like better than coming home from school and having Cheerio lick my face like it's a grape lollipop.

Unfortunately, Cheerio is not the only Zipzer family pet. My sister, Emily, who is a major reptile lover, has an iguana named Katherine. Katherine and Emily are a lot alike. They both have scales, they both hiss when they're mad, and they both get in bad moods about every four seconds. Oh, and they both eat parsley, which is that little green thing they put on the edge of your plate in a restaurant that no one ever eats. If you've never tasted it, take my advice and don't.

Here are a few lists that will give you an idea of just how cute Cheerio is, and just how un-cute Katherine is . . .

The Five Worst Things about Katherine

1. At dinner, she snatches all the carrots out of my soup with her long, sticky tongue. From now on, I'm switching to split pea.

2. Her breath smells like a three-day-old fish, and that's *after* we've brushed her teeth.

3. The newspaper at the bottom of her cage is covered with so many iguana droppings, you can't even see the baseball scores in the sports section.

4. When she swims in my bathtub, she leaves a reptile ring around the tub.

5. Iguanas can live for twenty years, which means Katherine will still be around when I'm thirty years old. I hope I'm out of the fifth grade by then.

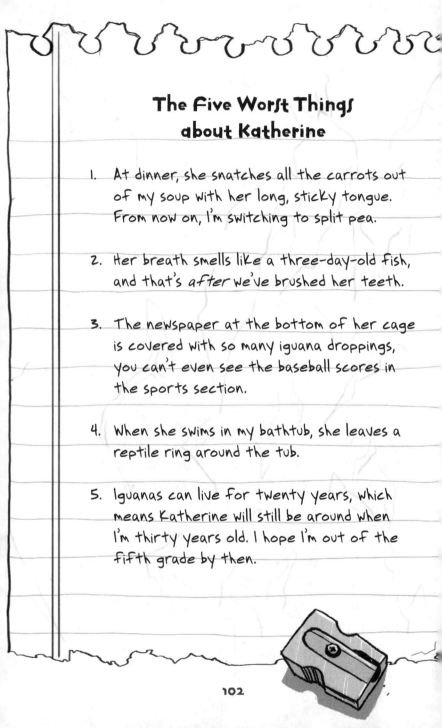

Emily and Katherine's Three Favorite Reptile Jokes

1. Knock knock. Who's there? Iguana. Iguana who? *Iguana hold your hand.*

2. What kind of tiles can't you stick on walls? *Reptiles!*

3. Where do frogs leave their hats and coats? *In the croakroom!*

Hey, I understand if you're not holding your sides and cracking up right now. Personally, I don't find reptile humor all that funny, either, but it makes my sister and her lizard laugh until their scales fall off. I told you they were weird.

Ten Really Creepy Facts Emily Has Told Me about Reptiles

1. Geckos are born without eyelids. They use their long tongues to lick their eyeballs to keep them from drying out.

2. Some horned lizards can squirt blood from their eyes when they're angry.

3. Chameleons are able to move and focus their eyes separately, so they can see in two directions at once.

4. An alligator's jaws are so strong they can bite through a turtle shell like it's a chocolate-chip cookie.

5. The world's longest snake, the reticulated python, can stretch himself to be taller than a three-story house.

6. A crocodile is unable to stick out his tongue.

If you'll excuse me now, I have to go in the corner of my room and scream. All this reptile talk is giving me a major case of the creeps. You'll have to find out the last four facts on your own.

Ten Things I Miss about Cheerio When I'm Not with Him

1. His brown eyes that look at me and say, Hank, buddy, I can't believe you're not sharing your steak with me!

2. His long hot-dog body that is so close to the ground, he could walk under my bed on his tiptoes if he wanted.

3. The way he is absolutely positive he's a big dog, even though he's not.

4. His floppy ears that perk up when he hears the *SpongeBob SquarePants* theme song on TV.

5. The way his bottom teeth stick out over his top teeth to make him look like he's smiling at you upside down.

6. The way he looks like a Cheerio when he chases his tail and spins in a circle.

7. The way he snarls at Katherine when she *isn't* having a hissy fit.

8. The way his little claws click on the linoleum when he's cruising around the kitchen looking for leftovers, which is most of the time.

9. The way he drops his favorite golf ball at my feet and looks at me as if to say, Any chance for a catch, pal?

10. A million billion other things that are all so cute if I mention them I swear I'll start to cry.

bark bark
bark
bark

Eight Naughty Things Cheerio Did at the Park

1. He chased a squirrel up a tree—that is, as far as Cheerio can go up a tree, which is about an inch.

2. He did a belly flop in the fountain and scared all the goldfish that thought he was Godzilla Dog.

3. He chased a flock of pigeons until they took off. He tried to flap his legs as if they were wings, and went exactly nowhere. No surprise.

4. He attached himself to Papa Pete's tracksuit and tugged so hard he almost pulled his pants down. (I never knew Papa Pete wore racing-car boxers!)

5. He jumped into an empty baby stroller, swiped the baby's rattle, stood up on his hind legs, and did the cha-cha.

6. He fell in love with a miniature schnauzer that, for some reason, was wearing four little red rain boots—and it wasn't even raining.

7. He peed on six rocks, nine shrubs, five lampposts, one fire hydrant, and one little old lady who didn't notice until it was too late.

8. I can't go on with this list, because I got so mad at him that when he ran up to me, I stepped on his leash, picked him up, and said, "That's it, we're going home."

Cheerio's Eight Favorite
Non-Dog-Food Treats

1. Crispy bacon. That's my favorite treat, too, especially when it's so well-done it's almost burned, but not quite. Uh-oh, my mouth is watering.

2. Orange Popsicles. He likes to lick the sticks while I try to read him the jokes. (His favorite one is: *How do pigs talk? Swine language!*)

3. Those little carrots that come in a bag. It's hilarious to listen to him crunch.

4. Peanut butter. When he tries to get it off the roof of his mouth, he looks like he's actually talking. (I bet he's saying, *Hey, you guys, you forgot the jelly!*)

5. My dad's slippers. He doesn't realize they're not food.

6. Chinese fortune cookies. He spits out the fortune inside because, like me, he can't read very well.

7. The couch legs. (See number five above.)

8. All of our dinner leftovers, which there are always a lot of because my mom's cooking tastes more like a science experiment than dinner.

One day, we took Cheerio to the senior center so he could play with the people there. He did not behave himself. And that's the biggest understatement in the history of the world.

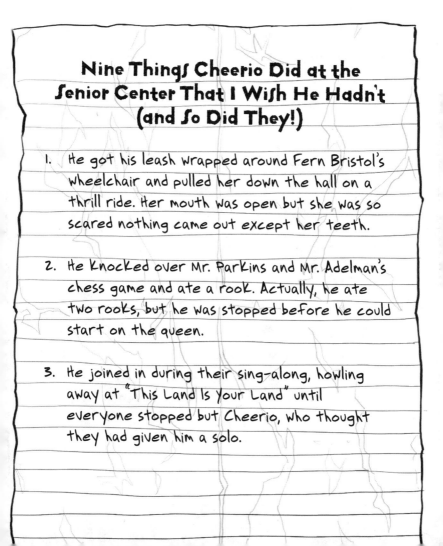

Nine Things Cheerio Did at the Senior Center That I Wish He Hadn't (and So Did They!)

1. He got his leash wrapped around Fern Bristol's wheelchair and pulled her down the hall on a thrill ride. Her mouth was open but she was so scared nothing came out except her teeth.

2. He knocked over Mr. Parkins and Mr. Adelman's chess game and ate a rook. Actually, he ate two rooks, but he was stopped before he could start on the queen.

3. He joined in during their sing-along, howling away at "This Land Is Your Land" until everyone stopped but Cheerio, who thought they had given him a solo.

4. He stuck his snout in Mr. Davis's trombone, and when Mr. Davis blew a high note, Cheerio's long, floppy ears shot straight up to the ceiling.

5. He got into the kitchen and ate 183 cups of applesauce and four chocolate puddings, and burped for the rest of the afternoon. Mrs. Carew kept asking, "Are we in an orchard?"

6. He snatched Mr. Hudnut's straw hat and peed on it so much the straw got all soggy and I spent the next half hour airing it out with a hair dryer.

7. He wouldn't stop licking Mrs. Chow's elbows because she uses a lotion that is scented with coconuts. She told him, "Beat it, pal. You're barking up the wrong tree."

8. He got into the art supplies, and let's just say the art room at the senior center is now a red room.

9. He tried to play with a goldfish in the aquarium and scared that poor fish so much, it jumped out of its tank and down Mrs. Witt's blouse. It was never found again.

Frankie, Ashley, and I tried to train Cheerio to do lots of tricks so he could enter a dog competition. He tried really hard and I give him credit for that. But in the end, he's my dog, and learning new things is just not what we're best at.

Five Things Cheerio Almost Learned

1. He *almost* learned to roll over, but stopped midway on his back and insisted on waving all four of his feet to air them out.

2. He *almost* learned to sit up on his hind legs, but kept falling over because his top part is longer than his bottom part.

3. He *almost* learned to snatch a Frisbee out of the air, but every time he was about to catch it, he'd just sit down and lick his tail.

4. He *almost* learned to walk with his head held high on a leash, but instead he grabbed the leash in his teeth and pulled Frankie into the birdbath, at which time the training was over because Frankie's mom took him right home to change his clothes so he wouldn't catch a cold. (You can only imagine the steam coming out of Frankie's mom's ears.)

5. Ashley made him a rhinestone crown that he *almost* learned to wear, but instead he shook it off his head, grabbed it in his mouth, ran to the bank of the Hudson, and flung it in the river. (I have to say, I'm on Cheerio's side on this one. Come on, he's not a rhinestone kind of guy.)

This is a bonus point on the list because it's not something Cheerio almost learned, but it's something *we* learned: Cheerio is definitely not a competition kind of dog.

Eleven Things I Always Say to Cheerio

1. Atta boy.

2. You're such a good puppy.

3. Who wants a belly rub?

4. Who wants his ears scratched?

5. Cheerio, go fetch!

6. That's okay, I can't catch, either.

7. Down, boy.

8. I said, Down, boy.

9. Come on, Cheerio, get down.

10. Cheerio, I'm not kidding. Get down.

11. Atta boy.

Sixteen Topics for Your Own Lists

Since I like to write lists so much, I thought you might enjoy it, too. Here are some list topics I thought would be fun. Oh, I know it says there are going to be sixteen topics and I ended up with nineteen. It was so much fun thinking about these, I just couldn't stop myself.

Ten Things I Would Change about My Mom and Dad If I Could

1.

2.

3.

4.

5.

6.

7.

8.

9.

10.

Eight Rules I Would Make My Brother or Sister Follow

1.

2.

3.

4.

5.

6.

7.

8.

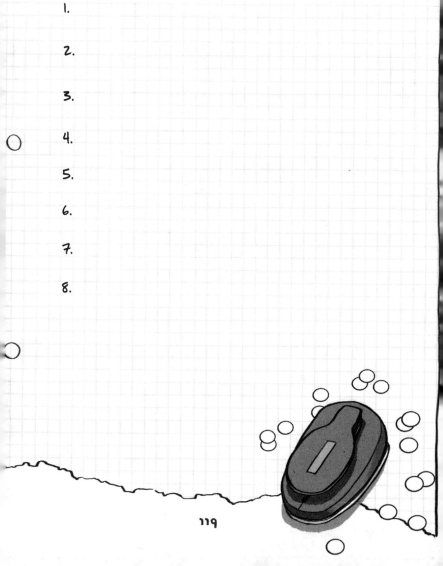

Seven Animals I Would Like to Be

1.

2.

3.

4.

5.

6.

7.

Six Things I Would Like
My Sweatshirts to Say

1.

2.

3.

4.

5.

6.

Five Superpowers I Wish I Had

1.

2.

3.

4.

5.

Three Strange Things
about My Toenails

1.

2.

3.

Six Pets I Would Like to Have

1.

2.

3.

4.

5.

6.

Three Snowy Places
I Would Like to Visit

1.

2.

3.

Six Silly Words I Just Made Up

1.

2.

3.

4.

5.

6.

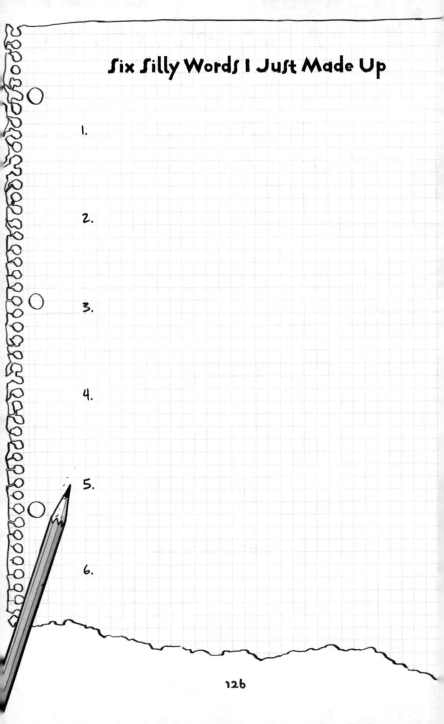

Nine Foods I Never Want to Eat

1.

2.

3.

4.

5.

6.

7.

8.

9.

Three Talents I Have and
Three Talents I Wish I Had

I Have

1.

2.

3.

I Wish I Had

1.

2.

3.

Ten Things I Would Say to a Dragon If I Met One

1.

2.

3.

4.

5.

6.

7.

8.

9.

10.

Six Things to Say After You Burp

1.

2.

3.

4.

5.

6.

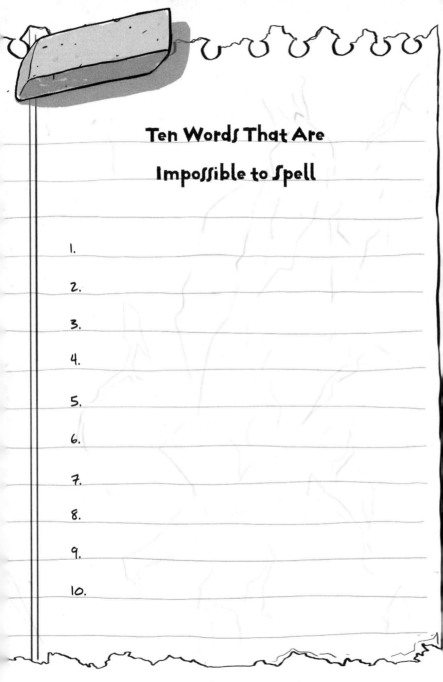

Ten Words That Are
Impossible to Spell

1.

2.

3.

4.

5.

6.

7.

8.

9.

10.

Seven Things I Always Lose

1.

2.

3.

4.

5.

6.

7.

Five Weird Things
I Can Do With My Tongue

1.

2.

3.

4.

5.

The Six Most Disgusting
Kinds of Cupcakes

1.

2.

3.

4.

5.

6.

Six Excellent Reasons to
Wear Clothes and One Silly One

1.

2.

3.

4.

5.

6.

7.

Nine Things My Socks Would Say If They Could Talk

1.

2.

3.

4.

5.

6.

7.

8.

9.

Well, that's it for *My Book of Pickles . . . Oops, I Mean Lists.* Speaking of pickles, I think I'll go have one. And I don't have to make a list about What I Like Best about Pickles, because the answer is EVERYTHING!!!!! I hope you liked everything about this book!

Your friend,

Hank "the Pickle" Zipzer

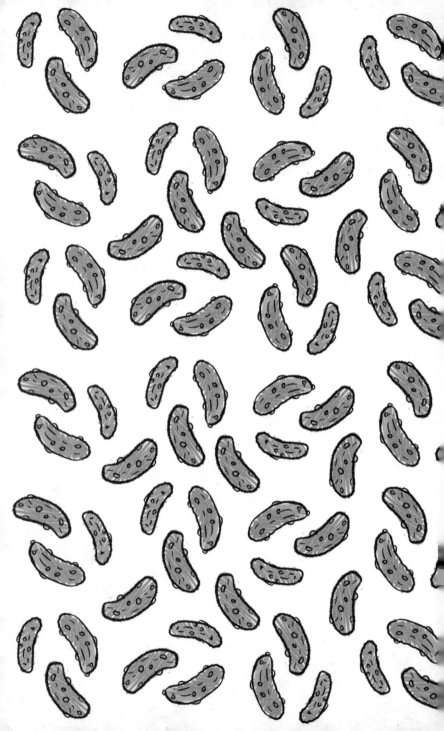